Dear Parents and Educators,

Welcome to Penguin Young Readers! As parents and educators, you know that each child develops at his or her own pace—in terms of speech, critical thinking, and, of course, reading. Penguin Young Readers recognizes this fact. As a result, each Penguin Young Readers book is assigned a traditional easy-to-read level (1–4) as well as a Guided Reading Level (A–P). Both of these systems will help you choose the right book for your child. Please refer to the back of each book for specific leveling information. Penguin Young Readers features esteemed authors and illustrators, stories about favorite characters, fascinating nonfiction, and more!

## A Pig, a Fox, and a Box

LEVEL 2

GUIDED READING LEVEL H

This book is perfect for a **Progressing Reader** who:

- can figure out unknown words by using picture and context clues;
- can recognize beginning, middle, and ending sounds;
- can make and confirm predictions about what will happen in the text; and
- can distinguish between fiction and nonfiction.

Here are some **activities** you can do during and after reading this book:

- Picture Clues: Use the pictures to tell the story. Have the child go through the book, retelling the story just by looking at the pictures.
- Make Predictions: At the end of this story, Fox is finished tricking Pig for the day. Do you think Fox will try to trick Pig again tomorrow? What do you think he will do?

Remember, sharing the love of reading with a child is the best gift you can give!

—Bonnie Bader, EdM
Penguin Young Readers program

*Penguin Young Readers are leveled by independent reviewers applying the standards developed by Irene Fountas and Gay Su Pinnell in *Matching Books to Readers: Using Leveled Books in Guided Reading*, Heinemann, 1999.

For Chad, Christopher, Amanda,
Michael, Katie, and Gregory.
Fine siblings all—JF

PENGUIN YOUNG READERS
Published by the Penguin Group
Penguin Group (USA) LLC, 375 Hudson Street, New York, New York 10014, USA

USA | Canada | UK | Ireland | Australia | New Zealand | India | South Africa | China

penguin.com
A Penguin Random House Company



Library of Congress Control Number: 2014044337

ISBN 978-0-448-48510-2 (pbk) 10 9 8 7 6 5 4 3
ISBN 978-0-448-48511-9 (hc) 10 9 8 7 6 5 4 3 2 1

PENGUIN YOUNG READERS

by Jonathan Fenske

Penguin Young Readers
An Imprint of Penguin Group (USA) LLC

# PART ONE

I am little.
I am big.

I have a box.
I like to play.
I think I will trick
Pig today.

I lift the lid.
I step inside.

I like to play.
I like to hide.

Oh, Pig, come here!
Oh, Pig, come see!

Did I just hear
Fox call for me?

I look around.
I see no Fox.
I only see a little box.

**So I will sit on this small box. And I will wait for little Fox.**

1.

2.

3.

The box went *BOOM*!
And I went *PLOP*!

Hee-hee.
I think I broke the box.
The box is flat.

And so is Fox.

# PART TWO

He is Fox.
He is Pig.

He is little.
He is big.

I have a wig.
I have some rocks.
Oh, I am such a sneaky fox!

I put the wig under
the rocks . . .

and hide inside
my little box.

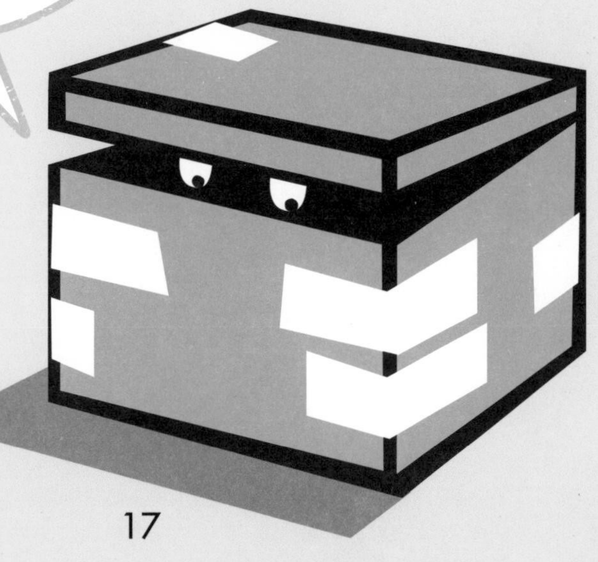

Help, help, big Pig!
Oh help!
Come see!

Did I just hear
Fox call for me?

But what is that?
It looks like Fox!

**Oh, this is BAD.
Poor little Fox
is under that big
pile of rocks!**

I will lift the rocks.
I will throw them far.
I am coming, Fox!
Stay where you are!

Uh-oh.

But what is this?
This is a wig.

Oh, I am such
a silly pig.

That big, big pile
of heavy rocks
was on a wig,
not on a fox.

Help, help, big Pig!
Oh help!
Come see!
There is a pile of
rocks on me!

He likes to play.
He makes me mad.

I see the rocks.
But this smart pig
knows that is just
another wig.

I will leave the wig.
I will leave the rocks.

This wig is flat.

And so is Fox.

# PART THREE

I am Fox.
I am Pig.
Pig was here

I am little.
I am big.

I like to hide.
I like to play.
But I am done
with that today.